AF259227

Earlene Green Evans grew up in Arlington, Virginia where she attended public schools. She received a B.S. and a M.S. degree, and worked as a school librarian until she retired.

During her career, Earlene co-authored three educational books. They are *A Step Beyond: Multimedia Activities for Learning American History, Hidden Skeletons and Other Funny Stories,* and *3-D Displays for Libraries, Schools, and Media Centers.* In addition to writing, Earlene enjoys reading, sewing and playing the flute.

Earlene, the mother of two grown children and a grandson, lives in Henrico, Virginia with her husband, Alga.

To the 1958 graduates of Hoffman-Boston High School.
There, we planted unforgettable memories.

Earlene Green Evans

BACK TO THE '50S

Illustrated by
Dennis R. Winston

AUSTIN MACAULEY PUBLISHERS™

LONDON • CAMBRIDGE • NEW YORK • SHARJAH

Copyright © Earlene Green Evans 2024
Illustrated by Dennis R. Winston

All rights reserved. No part of this publication may be reproduced, distributed, or transmitted in any form or by any means, including photocopying, recording, or other electronic or mechanical methods, without the prior written permission of the publisher, except in the case of brief quotations embodied in critical reviews and certain other non-commercial uses permitted by copyright law. For permission requests, write to the publisher.

Any person who commits any unauthorized act in relation to this publication may be liable to criminal prosecution and civil claims for damages.

Ordering Information
Quantity sales: Special discounts are available on quantity purchases by corporations, associations, and others. For details, contact the publisher at the address below.

Publisher's Cataloging-in-Publication data
Evans, Earlene Green
Back to the '50s

ISBN 9781685626501 (Paperback)
ISBN 9781685626518 (ePub e-book)

Library of Congress Control Number: 2023920268

www.austinmacauley.com/us

First Published 2024
Austin Macauley Publishers LLC
40 Wall Street, 33rd Floor, Suite 3302
New York, NY 10005
USA

mail-usa@austinmacauley.com
+1 (646) 5125767

I extend my sincere appreciation to my old neighborhood and my high school in Arlington, Virginia. The closeness of the neighbors, the love, nurturing, and memorable activities and events, local, national and international inspired me to put those experiences into a book of poems. To the teenagers across the country, their parents, and all who tasted and enjoyed the sweet decade of the '50s, thank you!

Table of Contents

Overview

The '50s was a decade of black and white photographs and television. It was a time of acceptance, calmness, contentment, and conservatism. Technology, turmoil, and violence lay dormant, waiting to be awakened. During this decade, people were orderly in their dress, mannerism, and actions. They were able to handle problems. For most, economic success through jobs was basically the 'American Dream.' The goal of young people was to get married, purchase an affordable house, and have children.

Young people in the '50s would have been considered 'nerds' by today's standards. They were respectful to all, accepting social covenants without protests. They were loyal to America and trusted the traditional system of authority. Many, having served time in the military, were optimistic about the future. The '50s was a silent decade that promised the beginning of many memorable changes and events.

Chapter 1
The Good Neighborhood

The poems in chapter one reflect the easy living conditions and security of the average American neighborhood during the 1950s. A man's home was truly his castle. Crime rate was at a minimum. Residents of most neighborhoods were stable and deeply rooted. They cooperated and showed respect for each other. Everyone was affected in some way by whatever happened in the neighborhood.

Everyone shared without reservation or consequences in guiding and directing children and young adults to be good citizens. Young adults often took jobs to help the family financially. High morals, social and religious standards were a part of everyday living.

Salespeople such as the bread man, the ice man, the ice cream man and the milkman were needed and depended on in the neighborhood. They, along with the neighborhood grocery store, offered goods, services, and conveniences to all.

Mind Your Manners, Please

Say 'Yes, sir,' 'Please,' 'Thank you.'
Wherever you go, whatever you do
You are under constant inspection,
That charters your direction.

You're watched by many eyes,
Of neighbors who tell no lies.
They stop and correct you on the spot,
Then send you home to get a knot.

When adults are talking, you'd better wait,
Or they will surely set you straight.
Say 'Excuse me please,' only if you're sick,
If you're not, you'll get a lick.

And when you come to the table to eat,
Greet your parents before taking a seat.
Then say you liked the meal,
Even if eating it was an ordeal.

If you're late for church, quietly tip in.
Show others you have discipline.
If you engage in conversation,
You'll be labeled 'bad generation.'

It doesn't matter if you're young or old,
Parents' rules stand loud and bold.
To live a life of comfort and ease,
Mind your manners, please, please!

Walking Through the Neighborhood

Walking through our neighborhood,
Carrying bags as best I could.
Without cares on my mind,
Doing a chore I'd been assigned.

Walking at a leisure pace,
Not the object of a chase.
Feeling secure as I can be,
Of no harm coming to me.

Strolling the streets, not looking back,
Or having a mental heart attack.
Meeting neighbors as I go,
Crime here is a no-no!

Walking in our neighborhood,
Enjoying a life that is good.
The walk from my house to the store,
Is safe and pleasant from door to door.

Washing Clothes

Gather your soiled clothes and put them in a pile,
We have a chore that's really worthwhile.
The job is fun with the help of a daughter…
Add washing powder to a tub of warm water.
Separate the clothes, the dark from the light,
Use a little bleach to make the whites bright.
Pull the lever for the agitator to work,
We wonder if the machine is going berserk.
The moaning and shaking comes to a stop,
Now use the wringer located at the top.
Guide the clothes through rollers going around,
If your hand gets caught, you will make a loud sound.
Put a basket in place to catch the flattened clothes.
Drain dirty water from the tub with the hose,
Dip some clothes in starch before hanging on the line,
Outside, they get a gentle breeze and warm sunshine.
Lined like soldiers, pins grip the clothes,
Dancing in the wind, they make three long rows.
Our laundry is done and out of the way…
We will iron the clothes on another day.

Party Line

We have a telephone in our home,
Shared with a family whose name is Rome.
As the Romes live down the road,
We agreed to follow the telephone code.
We have a party line.

We can hear them, they can hear us,
We hang up the phone without a fuss,
And wait patiently for their talk to end,
Good neighbors don't want to offend.
Using the party line.

I pick up the receiver to make a call,
I hear Jimmy Rome talking baseball.
I ease the receiver on the hook,
And say, "Oh well, I'll read a book."
Sharing our party line.

I decide to give it another try,
When Pat Rome said, "Hi, sweetie pie."
I change my plans, I'll take a walk.
In the evening, I'll have my talk,
On our party line.

After dinner, when I start to speak,
Mrs. Rome is calling Sue's Boutique.
To pass the time, I'll dust the house,
After that, I'll iron my blouse,
Because we have a party line.

I pick up the phone and hear their dad,
By now, I'm feeling very sad.
"What should I do?" I shake my head.
I give up! I'm going to bed.
Tomorrow, I'll use the party line!

Our Friend, the Radiator

The radiator is our true friend.
I will describe it from end to end.
Its iron legs are thick and strong,
It is three feet tall and four feet long.
Its body is a curvy mass of pipe,
It stands firm, the proud type.
Daddy gets up before daybreak,
And turns its knobs before we wake,
To start it up for the day,
Its response is slow, a lazy delay.
Then water in its pipes begins to boil,
Its friendship to us is being loyal.
Each morning it greets us, one and all,
With a popping, grunting, wake-up call.
Throwing off its heat, outwitting the cold,
Making a warm and cozy household.
At breakfast, it watches as we eat,
Pleased we are warm from head to feet.
When our friend is barely warm,
We touch the iron and stroke its form.
But when it is heated to its peak,
It will burn our fingers and make us shriek.
It has a personality of its own.
Often, it wants to be left alone.
Grandma makes use of our friend,
To keep food hot, that's a trend.

Or even use it to get clothes dry,
Our radiator friend on which we relay…
Is so dear to the heart,
From it, we never want to part.

The Grocery Store

The neighborhood grocery store,
Is around the corner or right next door.
A place to visit, chat or buy,
Almost anything under the sky.

From aspirin to coffee, milk, tea or soap,
Cold cream, toothpaste, a long thick rope.
Clothespins, sliced bacon, a loaf of bread,
Everything for the newlywed.

Owned by a couple in the neighborhood,
The Millers do much more than they should.
They give us jobs and spending money,
And soft fresh buns topped with honey.

For moms with little cash to spend,
The grocer is a treasured friend.
When money is small and the bill is greater,
It is put 'on the book,' and stamped, 'Pay later.'

The Milkman

At the crack of dawn while most are in bed,
The rumbling of his truck jogs every sleepy head.
In all kinds of weather, the sound's the same,
Rattling glass bottles, it's the milkman's game.

He stops at each house on his route,
Up and down the street and roundabout.
As faithful as the sunrise, as precise as a chemist,
He takes empty bottles from stoops on his list.

Then replaces them with cold, Grade A milk,
Topped with thick cream as smooth as silk.
Notes are left if there's money to spare,
For extra items, a request that's rare.

A pound of butter, a dozen eggs or two,
He fills each order, and adds the cash due.
Milk, eggs, and butter for a dollar and a dime,
These for himself would mean working overtime.

MILK

The Ice Man

"Ice…ice…ice…"
His voice makes dogs bark and children run
Bare foot on the street in the scorching sun,
To greet the ice man every other day.
His truck is heard before coming our way.

The procession moves down the street,
With dogs and kids trailing in the heat.
His head turns, his eyes span,
Listening for the call, "Ice Man! Ice Man."
Over the putt putt engine, voices yell…
Who wants what is hard to tell.
Fifteen, twenty, thirty pounds for me.
He climbs from the truck to fill each plea.

Under a canvas is hidden merchandise,
Buyers stand in line for a piece of ice.
Fifteen, twenty, twenty-five cents from you,
Each takes a block and pays what is due.

Inside each icebox, ice rests on a tray
To keep food cold for another day.
Everyone is warned to close the door,
Or water will drip on the kitchen floor.
"Ice…ice…ice…"

The ice man continues his work,
Always looking, turning with a jerk.
Scanning, listening for a call to stop,
To sell his ware from a moving ice shop.

ICE

The Bread Man

Hurry outside as fast as you can!
This is the day for the bread man.
He yanks a cord on his truck,
That sounds like a quacking duck.

He lets us know he's on our street,
With lots of goodies for all to eat.
Will we buy bread, cakes, or pies?
They look delicious, pleasing our eyes.

Making a choice is a hard chore,
To spend the least, not a penny more.
Bread, a pound cake…staying in control,
A treat for the kids, a sweet jelly roll.

The bread man bows, and says, "Good day."
Climbs in his truck and drives away,
To sell more goodies from door to door,
In his old truck, the neighborhood store.

CORSO BREAD
CORSO
BREAD

The Ice Cream Man

The ice cream man comes every day,
Afternoon or evening while we play.
When we hear the familiar rings,
We stop our games and jump from swings,
And run inside as fast as we can,
To ask for coins for the ice cream man.
It might be Good Humor or Jack & Jill…
We always get the same thrill,
Of spending coins our parents gave,
To buy delicious ice cream we crave.
With speedy legs and coins in hand,
We catch up with the ice cream man.
We make a choice, then change our minds,
There is ice cream, all different kinds!
The ice cream man is patient and nice,
He lets us choose according to price…
Dixie cups, Choc Cows, popsicles for licks,
The choice is made, we'll buy drumsticks!

ICE CREAM

Jobs for Teenagers

James has a job.
James needs some cash,
James has a job taking out trash.

Frank got a job
For the very first time,
Frank stacks shelves at the Five and Dime.

On Sherman's job, they wear name tags.
Sherman stays busy
Putting groceries in bags.

Earl's new job brings him joy.
Earl is a dependable
Newspaper boy.

Ricky has a job that you would like.
Ricky makes deliveries
Riding on a bike.

Barbara has a job helping her mom,
Doing household chores
To get a dress for the prom.

Freddie is a worker, he's no whiner.
Freddie washes dishes
At a local diner.

Clarence wants to take a trip with his class.
Clarence makes his money
Cutting neighbors' grass.

John needs money to pay his club dues.
John earns his money
Shining peoples' shoes.

Gwen has the job of everyone's dream.
Gwen works at the drugstore
Dipping ice cream.

Kids work after school, some otherwise.
Fifty cents an hour
Is a great compromise!

Chapter 2
Gather Around,
Sight and Sound

The poems in chapter two give an account of the use and effect of radio and television in the 1950s. Until the early 1950s, radio broadcasting had great influence on millions of families. Family members gathered around the radio to listen to dramas, comedies, variety shows and live music. The radio was an important source of audio communication.

Television was developed in the 1920s, but it did not become a part of most households in the United States until the 1950s. It brought picture and sound into the home from distant places. Programs included dramas, comedies, soap operas, sporting events, cartoons, quiz and variety shows, and motion pictures. Radio and television had been satisfying media for supplying information and entertainment to homes during the 1950s. However, many people were fascinated with, and favored picture and sound rather than just sound. Consequently, the radio lost many fans to the television.

The popularity of the television resulted in families and neighbors gathering to watch programs. Sales for televisions sets soared. Television was also a mean of escape. Many viewers ignored serious matters such as the threat of war or communism. By 1959, the average family was sitting in front of the television about six hours a day, seven days a week.

Neighborhood Television

The Greens bought a television set,
It cost so much, they are deep in debt.
A wooden box with a small round screen,
Showed pictures like a movie machine.
No other family in our neighborhood,
Could see stars in Hollywood.
We received the Greens' invitation,
To join a viewing celebration.
We gladly accepted and rushed next door,
Neighbors were sitting all over the floor.
The large crowd squeezed one another,
Lacking air, we thought we would smother.
Bodies were twisted, and turned just right,
To behold a show in black and white.
Eyes bulged and mouths dropped wide,
To see what a TV would provide.
The Lone Ranger chased a mean outlaw,
We joined the action with a big, "Hurrah!"
He took out his lasso, aimed it and threw,
As zigzag lines interrupted our view.
Mr. Green turned knobs from left to right,
The lines on the screen were an awful sight.
We were calm and patient; we had to wait.
After a while, the picture was straight.
The lasso missed as the picture started to roll,
This interruption was harder to control.
Frustrated, Mr. Green turned different knobs,
We shifted, squirmed, and suppressed our sobs.

When the rolling stopped, we read on the screen,
Words that could spark a mad mob scene.
The message was clear, it made us shriek…
"Tune in to The Lone Ranger again next week!"

Watching the Radio

We sit in a circle with the radio in view,
For hearing the precious sounds it threw,
Each listener has a ringside seat,
To imagine programs that can't be beat.
The family, plus the dogs and cats,
Sit in chairs or lay on mats,
To hear shows we long to see,
A mental picture is really the key.
Tonight, it's a pro boxing match,
Each plans to win without a scratch.
Who will succeed is a mystery,
This contest will make history.
We hear the announcer loud and clear,
Each boxer's name receives a cheer.
Dad says a prayer without delay,
To keep the radio static away.
The Brown Bomber, champ for twelve years,
Will fight Rocky Marciano, showing no fears.
The match will start at the sound of the bell,
Who will triumph is hard to tell.
Can Joe Louis punch and regain his crown
From Rocky, the hardest slugger in town?
Many have tried to beat and unseat him,
Until tonight, the chances were slim.
Excitement is high through round four.
Dad gets up and paces the floor.
Granddaddy rocks on his folding chair,
And throws wild punches in the air.

We hear and experience the whole event,
The static free station is heaven sent.
The announcer's voice is loud and strong,
For one fighter, something went wrong.
It was round eight when the knockout came,
For anyone to lose was really a shame!
Rocky ended the Brown Bomber's comeback.
The fight is recorded in the *World Almanac*.

Milton Berle

On Tuesday nights, we watch TV
To see the Texaco Star emcee,
Opening with servicemen singing
About products the show is bringing.
Then 'Uncle Miltie' comes on stage,
In costumes, some considers an 'outrage.'
Sometimes as a thing, a woman, or a man,
He has a unique comedy plan.
He is funny, weird, and even bold,
He falls and tickles a household.
He wears dresses and takes pies in his face,
His personality is easy to embrace.
Texaco Theater is a hit from the start,
The comedy show holds the nation's heart.
Berle makes TV sales rise,
A 94.7 rating is no surprise.
A television superstar, Berle is the first,
For making people laugh, he is well versed.
The year is 1952,
Berle makes his TV debut.

American Bandstand

Millions of teens share afternoons,
Dancing to the latest hit tunes.
It's television's American Bandstand,
The most popular show across the land.
Hosted by a short haired man, Dick Clark,
Whose personality has a gentle spark.
Stars sing rock, rhythm and blues,
Teens dance in groups, some in twos.
The crave spread from west to east,
Singing and dancing never cease.
Hand jive, bop, cha-cha or slop,
An hour each day, the fun is nonstop.
Clark's youngsters adore him…
'Oldest Teenager' is his pseudonym.
He receives 50,000 letters a week,
Supporting the show that is unique.
It attracts many want to be singers,
Some became rock and roll swingers.
They owe their success to the host of the show,
Francis and Darin, each is a pro.
Connie's 'Who's Sorry Now?' is a smash.

Bobby tops the chart singing, "Splish Splash."
American Bandstand is making its mark,
Rock and roll thrives, thanks to Dick Clark!

AB
DICK CLARK

"It's Howdy Doody Time"

Eyes on the TV, kids sit still,
Ready for a trip to Doodyville,
Where puppets and humans do their job,
Howdy Doody's host is Buffalo Bob.
A freckled faced puppet in western clothes,
Is the star of the show as everyone knows.
He charms each peanut gallery girl and boy,
Who visits Doodyville, that town of joy.
Multi-beast Flub-a-Dub gives the show luster,
For daily laughs, it's grumpy Mr. Bluster.
Beautiful princess Summerfall Winterspring,
Makes every boy and girl cheer and sing.
Sister Heidi and Double Doody, her twin,
Share fun with Scuttlebutt, the sea captain.
Clarabell, the clown never makes a sound,
But gestures, toots a horn, and runs around.
'It's Howdy Doody Time,' the theme song,
Makes children and parents sing along,
Aiming to entertain and educate,
Airing on television in '48.

I Love Lucy

She has us laughing until we cry,
The bride of a handsome Cuban guy,
Together with landlords, Ethel and Fred,
The 'I Love Lucy' show is widespread.

On Monday nights, we sit to view,
What the redhead comedian, Lucy will do.
When bandleader hubby goes to work,
Her weird ideas begin to perk.

In trying to be the perfect wife,
She creates funny mix-ups in her life.
Her intentions are good, as all can see,
She is married to Desi off and on TV.

Wise Fred and Ethel give Lucy aid,
They add to the hilarious mess she has made.
When the mess explodes, and Ricky finds out,
He throws a fit and gives a shout.

The three confesses and tells the truth,
Now Ricky is sorry for acting uncouth.
Each episode ends with laughter and glee,
For Ricky Ricardo loves Lucy.

I LOVE LUCY

M-I-C-K-E-Y M-O-U-S-E

"Who's the leader of the gang?"
It started with a question and a bang!
M-I-C-K-E-Y M-O-U-S-E
Aired from '55 to '59 on national TV.

It was the Mickey Mouse Club, of course,
With Jimmie Dodd and a super task force,
Of children wearing mouse ears hats,
And first names T-shirts for young diplomats.

The Mouseketeers carried the show,
With singing and dancing to and fro.
Each day there was a different theme…
Guests or cartoons planned by the team.

With documentaries in between,
Kids learned while watching a TV screen.
Of thirty-nine kids who answered roll call,
Nine stayed and had a ball.

Sha-ron, Bob-by, Lon-nie, An-nette…
Displayed their talent on the set.
Tom-my, Ka-ren, Carl, Do-reen…
Eight Mouseketeers plus one, Dar-lene.

Their last 'Good-bye' was in '59,
But Mickey Mouse continues to shine,
In the hearts of children everywhere.
No other kids' show would compare!

JIMMIE
SHARON

Davy Crockett

In '54, TV generated a fad,
It got the attention of Mom and Dad.
Even Grandpa dug deep in his pocket,
To buy things labeled, 'Davy Crockett.'

Played by Fess Parker, a courageous man,
On Walt Disney's show, 'Disneyland.'
Millions of viewers from five to fifteen,
Watched their hero on the TV screen.

A famous frontiersman in the U.S.A.
Crockett fought Indians many a day.
He wrestled bears and escaped their claws,
And served as congressman and made laws.

A million-dollar market for his coonskin caps,
Swimsuits, lunch pails, and guitars with straps.
The 'Ballad of Davy Crockett' was high on the chart,
King of the wild frontier stole America's heart.

Soon Crockett's items piled in every store,
To kids, this crave began to bore.
The fad, short lived, was gone in a year…
Crockett was king of the wild frontier.

DAVY CROCKETT

Chapter 3
Looking Good,
Being Understood

Chapter three focuses on popular young people's fashion trends during the 1950s. In addition to being clean from head to feet, boys and girls wanted to make an impression on each other with a special touch. Many teenagers selected fads, including hairdos, they felt enhanced their looks and boosted their popularity among their peers. Although fashion trends during the '50s were very popular, most were short-lived. However, fashion and trend during that time created much excitement, attention, and caused the fashion industry to soar financially.

Nothing to Wear

My closet is full; I have nothing to wear,
To make an impression at the county fair.
I survey the rack from end to end,
Looking for clothes of the latest trend.
I have nothing to wear.

A green sack dress catches my eye.
The bow on the back does satisfy.
It will fit like a tube, hanging mid-calf,
But for the fair, what a laugh!
I have nothing to wear!

My full floral cotton skirt is in view,
I'd wear a crinoline slip or two.
My off-shoulder blouse will go well,
I would look like 'Mademoiselle.'
I have nothing to wear!

A pink skirt with a black poodle at the hem,
The fuzzy puppy head makes it a gem.
A poodle skirt is admired by many,
It cost Mom three dollars and a penny.
I have nothing to wear!

There! Looking at me…
As plain as my eyes can see,
My new pedal pushers in black,
Is my choice from the rack.
I found something to wear!

Hairstyles

Fad hairstyles weep north, south, east, and west,
The one you chose, you think is the best.
The short curly hair poodle covers the skull…
Without a pretty face, you'd look rather dull.

Bangs hanging longer than some hairdos,
Peep through strands for clear views.
Hair on the forehead, shaggy or straight,
With pigtails or ponytails, bangs go great!

The pageboy hairstyle graces the face.
Every strand of hair has its own place.
Straight, smooth, turned under at the ends,
A feminine message, the pageboy sends.

Some guys hop on the foul trail,
Their hairstyle is the ducktail.
Hair combed from the sides like a duck's rear,
Forms a furrow which causes a smear.

Shoes

The choice of shoes is pleasing to the eye,
At a price moms squeeze money to buy.
For everyday wear or Sunday school,
Caring for shoes is the home rule.

There are penny loafers in tan, black, or brown,
Worn by boys and girls all around town.
No shoestrings to tie, just slip on and go,
See a coin in a slot when you look below.

Saddle oxfords' two colors make a smashing hit,
Black and white will grace any outfit.
The string ups ensure non-slip strolls,
Some with leather, some with rubber soles.

I think mules will stay on my feet.
These bareback shoes are really neat.
No slipping or sliding, they fit just right,
With my new dress, I'll wear them tonight.

Billy Eckstine's Shirts

Billy Eckstine's hits are hot in 1950…
His soothing voice soars high on the chart.
Also known for his shirts, stylish and thrifty,
They attract men who are quite smart.
The pastel colors are fresh, soft, and new,
To impress a young man's sweetheart.
Pink, yellow, light green, or baby blue…
Long sleeves with buttons or fancy cuff links,
The wide oversized collar with a skinny tie,
Brings nods, smiles, and female winks.
Though many men do not look like Mr. B,
They follow the trend of the well-dressed guy…
Because what they wear is really the key.

Bermuda Shorts

They're too long for regular shorts,
Worn by many in various sports…
Too short for the normal slacks,
Some wear them just to relax.
The British Navy started this trend,
Now in the U.S.A., we have a new friend.
Popular in Bermuda, that got the name,
For work or leisure, the shorts gain fame.
Cotton, linen, wool, just to name a few,
Multiple colors and designs to satisfy you.
The legs are exposed from the knees to the feet,
Bermudas in America cannot be beat!
The widely loved shorts have passed the trial…
They have become a domestic style!
We'll look at the 50s years from now,
And hail Bermudas with a cheer and a "WOW!"

Crinoline Slips

What an amazing sight…
Teens displaying sheer delight.
Dressed like colonial dolls,
Gliding through the halls.

Across the nation in high schools,
Respecting regulations, policies, and rules,
Girls are wearing crinoline slips,
Stiffened by numerous starchy dips.

Claiming space like a formal ball gown,
They sit up when the girls sit down.
Portraying the lady, Queen Antoinette,
Hiding two slips underneath, I bet.

Ladies of old, have admirers indeed…
Wearing crinolines will proceed.
The girls of the '50s have captured your style.
Crinoline slips will be here for a while.

Chapter 4
News to Use or Refuse

During the '50s, it was common to hear a familiar singsong call from the newspaper boy, "Extra! Extra! Read All About it!" Whether it was important news or not, boys were 'pushing' newspapers. They were arousing excitement while trying to earn a few extra coins. Most readers were attracted to the headlines. However, local news, politics, sports, fashion, and music had a permanent place in the newspapers. These subjects captured the interest of numerous readers. No one wanted to miss anything printed that was newsworthy throughout the country and the world. For that reason, newspapers were in demand. Most single copies sold for about five cents.

Hail to the Queen of England

Hail to England's new queen!
She is young, attractive, and serene.
News from afar reached our shore,
Reporting King George lives no more.
George VI has passed; the account is sad.
Good-bye to Princess Elizabeth's beloved dad.
Now, the princess fills that void.
The royal family is overjoyed.
Monarch of Great Britain, Commonwealth of Nations,
Two of her numerous obligations.
In '53, Elizabeth began her reign,
Sir Philip at her side, he vowed to remain.
Serving her country beyond its call,
Queen Elizabeth II is hailed by all!

Richard Milhous Nixon

A pragmatic young man from a western state,
Dreamed of entering the political gate.
With a bold personality and energy galore,
Richard Milhous Nixon aimed to soar.
He deliberately planned to get to the top,
Starting at the bottom, not meaning to stop.
In 1950, he joined the elite group…
A U.S.A. senator, getting the inside scoop.
Not being satisfied, he pushed and spoke out loud,
As his Vice President, Eisenhower was proud.
The two made a team that couldn't be beat.
For two terms, Ike and Nixon kept the seat.
Then for president, Nixon battled JFK,
John whipped Richard and sent him away.
But Nixon stayed around to be kicked around,
And claimed presidency on the rebound.
For our country, he opened many a gate,
The gate that broke him yelled, "Checkmate!"

I Want to Be a Person of Fame

I want to be a person of fame,
Known widely by my name.
A singer, a dancer, a movie star,
To entertain people near and far.

Perhaps like Liz Taylor, the beautiful one,
Starred in the movie, *A Place in the Sun.*
She captures men with those violet eyes,
And marries not one, but many guys.

Ah, Lena Horne, lady of song,
Her acting skills are very strong.
She makes her operatic debut in '54,
Lena will be loved forevermore.

Frank Sinatra sings to groups large and small,
Whether ballad or rhythm, he renders them all.
The 'Voice,' the nickname spotlights his skills,
'Ole Blue Eyes' will give everyone a thrill.

I could imitate the velvety voice,
Of Nat King Cole, a favorite choice.
His 'Mona Lisa' is loved and sung,
The melody lingers on every tongue.

There is Marilyn Monroe, the blond fun girl,
She included Arthur and Joe in her world.
The wind up her skirt from a manhole…
A face remembered for a cute black mole.

Sammy Davis, Jr. can act and dance…
And thrill fans with songs of romance.
He is short, articulate, serious, and funny,
Mr. Davis makes lots of money.

Doris Day, a sweet actress and singer,
In 'Pajama Game,' she is a ringer!
Energetic, clean and fresh as a flower,
Her innocent smile gives her the power.

Harry Belafonte, the 'King of Calypso,'
Sings various music and puts on a show,
His folk songs touch us and make us sway,
His tunes in our heads won't go away.

I want to be a person of fame,
Today, I will start taking aim.
I'll be on the screen and in the news,
I believe I'll get great reviews!

Extra! Extra! Read All About It!

We dance in the streets with laughter and tears,
Harry Truman has solved our fears.
Ending the war was the President's plan,
He ordered, "Drop the bomb on Japan!"

Extra! Extra! Read all about it!
Rosa Parks is determined to sit,
On Alabama's bus in '55,
The movement started is still alive.

Extra! Extra! Read all about it!
Researchers for polio just won't quit.
Jonas Salk's vaccine in 1952,
Yields an amazing science breakthrough.

Extra! Extra! Read all about it!
They say nine students would not fit…
Escorted by guards to Central High,
At Little Rock, in the nation's eye.

Extra! Extra! Read all about it!
The islands of Hawaii make a hit,
Becoming a state in 1959,
Known for its beauty and warm sunshine.

EXTRA EXTRA...
READ ALL ABOUT IT.
ROSA PARKS
TAKES A SEAT!!

School Desegregation

The eyes of the world are on D.C.
This side of the ocean, land of the free.
Home of the United States Supreme Court,
Where monumental decisions are not a sport.

Will Black and White kids attend the same schools?
Or will they live by the laws of fools?
Black lawyers work to present their case…
Of segregation, a national disgrace.

Separate, but equal cannot proceed,
Equality, regardless of race or creed.
Spottswood Robinson, Thurgood Marshall, and Harold Boulware,
Aim to reverse racial laws, declaring them unfair.

They are key lawyers in Brown verses the Board.
This terrible situation will not be ignored!
A decision is made by the nine in black,
That segregationists are on the wrong track.

Now, every Black child in any public school,
Will benefit from this constitutional rule.
Thanks to the judges of the highest court,
Thanks to the lawyers who challenged and fought.

Race to Space

What a shock in October, 1957!
A Russian satellite soared toward heaven!
It was tiny, unmanned, but made big news.
How they did it, we have no clues.
Orbiting the earth, Sputnik claimed, "FIRST!"
Russia's pride would not be reversed.
AMERICA should be first to send a rocket up,
And maintain power, not a paper cup.
Have the Soviets gained the upper hand in science?
Will this affect friendship with other world giants?
Eisenhower speeds up our space program,
And launched a mighty grand slam…
In January, '58, Explorer I, without man,
Blasted off and the Space Race began!

Chapter 5
School Days, Knowledge Pays

Schools in the '50s were closely connected to the church and community activities. It definitely took a village to rear a child, and everyone was involved. Children were required and expected to follow school rules with few exceptions. Teachers were respected and held to the highest esteem. The school, the church, and the community consisted of one big family unit. This unit worked to educate the children, provide spiritual and moral upbringing and provide a healthy living environment. The unit, teachers, parents, and ministers cooperated and worked to obtain the desired goal. That goal resulted in a product of well-educated, high moral, successful students.

Our Teacher

Our teacher is classy, well-dressed, and smart,
Her attire is a creative work of art.
Wearing a suit, heels, gloves, and a matching hat,
She is a genuine aristocrat!
Once in the school, she makes a change,
Some might think this lady is strange!
Off goes the hat, gloves, and heels,
A smock over her suit protects and conceals.
She works at the blackboard and the hectograph machine,
When the bell rings, we start our daily routine.
First, the Pledge of Allegiance is said,
Then a patriotic song by a student is led.
Everyone recites by memory the health creed,
Said seriously and deliberately at a slow speed.
Our teacher checks our head, ears, neck, and teeth,
Then asks if everything is clean underneath.
Satisfied with every reply of "yes,"
We start our work and aim for success.

LESSON TODAY
SCIENCE!
Page 47-49

Our Class Work

Our dedicated teacher does not play,
She gets the most from us each day.
She tells us to make good use of our time.
Unfinished work is a childhood crime!
You might have to sit on the dunce stool…
And be punished at home for breaking the rule.
Our first reader is about Dick and Jane,
We learn to read by sight, using our brain.
Penmanship is forming letters just right,
Good handwriting is a welcome delight.
Adding, subtracting, dividing numbers,
Reciting timetables without stumblers.
We learn from our *Weekly Reader* magazine,
It is the best news source we have seen.
Our teacher introduces us to music and art,
We draw and paint using supplies from a cart.
We learn music notes and songs of the season,
And perform cantatas for no special reason.
At the end of the day, for home we walk,
Around the dinner table, it's mainly school talk,
About all we learned at school that day…
And not wanting our teacher to go away.

Fight at Recess

Recess at last! It's time for some fun.
Let's see which team is number one.
This baseball game is for boys only,
The losers will be sad and lonely.
Which team will prove to be the best?
The losers will have a long rest.
Let's finish the game we started yesterday…
And keep the scores play by play.
Will it be Frank's Brown Bears or Bill's Wild Cats?
The weak boys will scatter like scared rats.
Nobody wanted to hear the bell ring,
That means, 'STOP,' no matter who's up to swing.
The score is 5 to 4 in favor of Bill's team,
"We are the best!" Bill let out a scream.
"Let's finish tomorrow," Frank insisted.
"No, we are the best!" Bill's team resisted.
Frank gave Bill an unexpected push,
Bill fell backward into a thick bush.
Other children gathered and caused a loud noise,
Watching the fists of two angry boys.
The yelling stopped when the teacher appeared,
The boys dropped their fists, the others cleared,
All lined up and walked quietly inside,
Frank's and Bill's parents will be notified.
When class work was completed for the day,
Frank and Bill were told to stay.
They had to write 200 times,
Because fighting is one of the school's crimes.

They copied, *Fighting is for dogs and cats.*
Boys settle disputes with handshakes and pats.
They sat and wrote side by side,
By writing the sentence, they learned well,
The lesson about fighting as clear as a bell.
Each paper got a nod of satisfaction,
With a warning about their awful action.
Without being told, the boys shook hands.
Walking home, making new game plans.

Sock Hop

We're having a sock hop in the gym after school,
We'll do the latest dances and follow the rule…
Stay inside until the sock hop ends,
Don't go outside to meet late friends.
White socks, colored socks cover the floor,
Shoe wearers will be stopped at the door.
Everyone is seeking a partner to dance,
The shy and bashful won't have a chance!
The first song by the Drifters is 'Dance With Me,'
The gym floor is as crowded as it can be,
From the beginning, the affair is mighty nice,
Sparked by 'Stagger Lee,' the singer, Lloyd Price.
On other popular songs, we move nonstop,
We dance until we are about to drop.
Slow songs require space between the two,
Or just sit until that song is through.
It's the 'Uptown,' 'Mashed Potato,' 'Madison,' 'Bird Land,'
Our dancing skills are learned firsthand.
Move now is the wallflowers' last chance,
Bill Haley's 'See You Later Alligator' ends this dance.
As all good things must come to an end,
We look forward to the next sock hop we will attend.

The Prom

The time for the prom is finally here,
We waited for this special day all year.
My high fashioned gown of netted green…
Is the prettiest one I have seen.
My nylon stockings and mules will be great,
I'll look my best for my first real date.

A sparkling tiara gives me class,
I see a new me in the looking glass.
My date, my neighbor's handsome son,
Is approved by parents, saying, "He's the one!"
Steve knocks on my door at half past six,
Promising my dad, there will be no tricks.
He looks quite different in a formal suit,
I had to admit, this boy is cute!
He greets me with a smile and a wink,
And gives me a live corsage of pink.
Being too young to drive a car,
His dad drives us to school, not far.
We are greeted by teachers and classmates,
And urged to mingle with other prom dates.
This is the beginning of a wonderful night,
Students in their best make a lovely sight.
'Dance With Me,' 'Searchin,' 'The Stroll,'
Are our favorite dance songs of rock and roll.
The punch is fruity, the hors d' oeuvres are hot,
We do different moves, even the fox trot.
Every girl's gown is under the spotlight,

The grand march is lively and bright,
Before we know it, it's time to go.
The last song played is romantic and slow.
Out front, Steve's dad is already there,
To take us home from the memorable affair.
At my door, I get a peck on my cheek,
It happened so fast, I let out a squeak.

"Thank you and good night," I manage to say…
But he's in the car that's driving away.

Chapter 6
Lots of Fun for Everyone

The '50s was good clean fun! Everyone enjoyed themselves doing whatever they wanted to do within reason. Young people had so much enjoyment engaging in physical and low organizational sports and games, that adults often joined them. Children played hand-me-down games such as dodge ball, Statues, Red Light, Mother, May I, and kick ball. They also had a love for ring games such as Ring Around the Rosie, London Bridge, Little Sally Ann, and Bluebird In and Out the Window. Favorites on the front stoops and sidewalks were checkers, jack rocks, and hopscotch. The hula-hoop fad swept across America and people of all ages hopped on. This was excellent recreational and physical exercise.

Boys constructed and used slingshots or bean shooters for hunting in the woods. They climbed trees and swam in swimming holes. For fun and excitement, adults often formed baseball teams and competed against each other. Children and other adults observed and cheered.

Boys and girls danced to rock and roll and rhythm and blues music. This kept them occupied and physically fit. Car transportation was scarce; therefore, everyone walked almost everywhere without complaining.

Life in the '50s was innocent, sweet, delightful, entertaining, and virtually worry free. What a fun filled way to live!

95

Singing Under the Lamp Post

The evening is young, the chores are done,
We're singing under the lamp post, having fun.
A quartet of young men blending one voice,
Performing popular songs of their choice.
Harmonizing, swaying, and stepping in time,
The ladder of stardom, they're striving to climb.
Vocalizing like top groups on the radio,
Aspiring to be on the Ed Sullivan's Show.
Often accompanied by a single guitar,
Serious entertainment could take them far.
Echoing the Drifters, the Diamonds and the Platters,
Making an impression is all that matters.
By luck, their notes reach a pro's ear,
Who offers a deal for a music career.
The youngsters score high in rock & roll,
What a break for boys singing under a pole!
Other groups, trying to succeed claim a space,
Searching for that dream of which to chase.
Singing and swinging the doo wop way,
Their music gets better day by day.
The lamp post gives energy and confidence,
Working for a cause, it makes good sense!

The Drive-In Theater

The drive-in movies have again started,
From home to the movie, we departed.
On warm summer nights, we sit in the car,
And view motion pictures and news from afar.

The charge for the movie is by the car load,
Therefore, a car full will not mean much owed.
My family, Mom, Dad, my brothers and me,
Park the car where we can all see.

Dad gets the speaker and puts it in the window,
And adjusts the volume neither too high nor too low.
Mom and I get food from the stand…
Buttered popcorn and soda pop as we planned.

When the sun starts to set, the news is first,
Followed by cartoons, creating a huge outburst.
The feature is 'Tarzan, Lord of the Jungle.'
He scales trees without a bungle.

Big game hunters arrive in canoes,
Looking for animals whose hide they could use.
There's a fight; Tarzan and Jane against the men…
With the help of Cheetah and every jungle friend.

The hunters' guns make a loud noise,
But friend gorilla toss them like toys.
We yell and cheer to the bitter end,
The beaten hunters decide to descend.

They jump in the river to swim away,
But hungry alligators catch their prey…
Tarzan and friends celebrate with joy,
They stopped the hunters' aim to destroy.

The words, 'The End,' appear on the screen,
And off goes the sound on the movie machine.
Dad puts the speaker back in place,
And we leave our drive-in parking space.

House Party

There's a teen house party on Friday night,
We move to music under a blue light.
Mary's basement is a cozy place,
This room downstairs has limited space.

Will that stop us from cutting a rug?
Not as long as the cord stays in the plug.
We bump each other, but we don't mind,
Doing the 'Mashed Potato,' and that forbidden 'Grind.'

The 'Uptown,' and the 'Bird Land' are favorites, too,
Performed by members of a rock and roll crew.
A scratched record makes as an ugly repeat,
Moving the head forward makes the song complete.

Refreshments are provided by Pam and Jade,
We have homemade cookies and lime Kool Aid.
Everyone stops for a kissing game,
'Spin the Bottle' and kiss your 'flame.'

Dancing continues, fast and slow,
Cheers to the couple who takes the floor.
The party is fun until Mary's parents appear,
And remind us that the end is near.

On the last record, we do a slow-moving dance,
And steal a little kiss, taking a chance.
Then tell Mary, our house party host,
We enjoyed the evening to the upmost!

Saturday Evening Movies

At the recreation center each Saturday night,
We see exciting movies in black and white.
Money is earned after school each day,
To see actors in places far away.
Mr. Smith gives a quarter for cutting his grass,
I will see the movie with friends from my class.
Twenty-five cents is collected at the door,
We have snacks bought from the store.
We sit in a room of chairs and a screen,
And wait for the sound of the movie machine.
Our favorite seats are on the front row,
For a clear view of the picture show.
All of a sudden, the room is black,
We yell and scream as if being attacked.
Screams turn to cheers as we see Bugs Bunny,
The crazy things he does are very funny.
Bugs Bunny cartoon comes to an end,
Now, we see Lassie, man's best friend.
Lost in the forest to wander and roam,
We want Lassie to find her way home.
The smart dog finds those who love her,
They hug her and brush her matted fur.
We applaud the ending of Lassie who was lost.
She was determined to get home at any cost.
Next week's feature will be hero, 'Zorro,'
Twenty-five cents will get me through the door.

TARZAN

Tree Fun

There is never a bad time for climbing trees,
As long as you don't disturb angry bees.
There are elms, maples, sycamores and oaks,
From which to look at strolling folks.
The closet maple is our choice today,
To bad weather, please stay away!
I climb to a limb that supports my weight,
Relaxing up high will be just great.
I settle and balance my body to rest…
When I hear my name being addressed.
Peeping through leaves, who do I see?
Billy in the next tree calling me.
He has his best loved comic book boys,
Archie and Jughead out rate many toys.
Billy made the climb before I got here,
He was reading and enjoying the atmosphere.
We talk, laugh, and appreciate the breeze,
There's nothing like being high in the trees.
After a while, we carefully climb down…
From a favorite place in our hometown.
Tomorrow, we will climb trees near the lake,
Share comic books and Mom's chocolate cake.

Fun in All Seasons

How we welcome summer's warm touch!
The fun-filled days are enjoyed so much.
School is out, we take off our shoes,
Walk through the grass or wherever we choose.
Net a butterfly and catch a firefly,
Then let them go to again fly high.
On the Fourth of July, we celebrate galore,
Our nation's birthday as never before!

Autumn appears with a chill in the air,
Time for school, lessons, and the county fair.
Beautiful leaves fall by the millions,
Making a colorful carpet of perhaps billions.
Now, fun on the leafy hill begins,
We cover each other up to our chins.
Sliding downhill on a piece of cardboard,
Is the only ride we can afford.

Snow falls before Thanksgiving Day,
We get the old sled and go out to play.
Sliding down the snow-covered hill,
A piggyback ride gives a double thrill.
Some riders fall off and roll down,
The steepest hill in our little town.
We stop when our mittens are full of snow,
Then, inside we go for hot cocoa.

The downpour of the spring rain begins to cease,
A beautiful rainbow appears in the east.
Puddles and tiny streams are here and there,
We stomp and splash water everywhere.
Laughing, splashing, and enjoying being wet,
Moving through puddles before sunset.
"Children," Mom calls, "that is enough!"
Leaving the puddles is really tough.

Index

www.ingramcontent.com/pod-product-compliance
Lightning Source LLC
Chambersburg PA
CBHW061743050726

47598CB00002B/573